The Poor Clare

ELIZABETH CLEGHORN GASKELL

Published in 1896

TABLE OF CONTENTS

THE POOR CLARE

THE POOR CLARE

CHAPTER I.

December 12th, 1747.—My life has been strangely bound up with extraordinary incidents, some of which occurred before I had any connection with the principal actors in them, or indeed, before I even knew of their existence. I suppose, most old men are, like me, more given to looking back upon their own career with a kind of fond interest and affectionate remembrance, than to watching the events— though these may have far more interest for the multitude— immediately passing before their eyes. If this should be the case with the generality of old people, how much more so with me! . . . If I am to enter upon that strange story connected with poor Lucy, I must begin a long way back. I myself only came to the knowledge of her family history after I knew her; but, to make the tale clear to any one else, I must arrange events in the order in which they occurred—not that in which I became acquainted with them.
There is a great old hall in the north-east of Lancashire, in a part they called the Trough of Bolland, adjoining that other district named Craven. Starkey Manor-house is rather like a number of rooms clustered round a gray, massive, old keep than a regularly-built hall. Indeed, I suppose that the house only consisted of a great tower in the centre, in the days when the Scots made their raids terrible as far south as this; and that after the Stuarts came in, and there was a little more security of property in those parts, the Starkeys of that time added the lower building, which runs, two stories high, all round the base of the keep. There has been a grand garden laid out in my days, on the southern slope near the house; but when I first knew the place,

the kitchen-garden at the farm was the only piece of cultivated ground belonging to it. The deer used to come within sight of the drawing-room windows, and might have browsed quite close up to the house if they had not been too wild and shy. Starkey Manor-house itself stood on a projection or peninsula of high land, jutting out from the abrupt hills that form the sides of the Trough of Bolland. These hills were rocky and bleak enough towards their summit; lower down they were clothed with tangled copsewood and green depths of fern, out of which a gray giant of an ancient forest- tree would tower here and there, throwing up its ghastly white branches, as if in imprecation, to the sky. These trees, they told me, were the remnants of that forest which existed in the days of the Heptarchy, and were even then noted as landmarks. No wonder that their upper and more exposed branches were leafless, and that the dead bark had peeled away, from sapless old age.

Not far from the house there were a few cottages, apparently, of the same date as the keep; probably built for some retainers of the family, who sought shelter—they and their families and their small flocks and herds—at the hands of their feudal lord. Some of them had pretty much fallen to decay. They were built in a strange fashion. Strong beams had been sunk firm in the ground at the requisite distance, and their other ends had been fastened together, two and two, so as to form the shape of one of those rounded waggon- headed gipsy-tents, only very much larger. The spaces between were filled with mud, stones, osiers, rubbish, mortar—anything to keep out the weather. The fires were made in the centre of these rude dwellings, a hole in the roof forming the only chimney. No Highland hut or Irish cabin could be of rougher construction.

The owner of this property, at the beginning of the present century, was a Mr. Patrick Byrne Starkey. His family had kept to the old faith, and were stanch Roman Catholics, esteeming it even a sin to marry any one of Protestant descent, however willing he or she might have been to embrace the Romish religion. Mr. Patrick Starkey's father had been a follower of James the Second; and, during the disastrous Irish campaign of that monarch he had fallen in love with an Irish beauty, a Miss Byrne, as zealous for her religion and for the Stuarts as himself. He had returned to Ireland after his escape to France, and married her, bearing her back to the court at St. Germains. But some licence on the part of the disorderly gentlemen who surrounded King James in his exile, had insulted his beautiful wife, and disgusted him; so he removed from St. Germains to Antwerp, whence, in a few years' time, he quietly returned to Starkey Manor- house—some of his Lancashire neighbours having lent their good offices to reconcile him to the powers that were. He was as firm a Catholic as ever, and as stanch an advocate for the Stuarts and the divine rights of kings; but his religion almost amounted to asceticism, and the conduct of these with whom had been brought in such close contact at St. Germains would little bear the inspection of a stern moralist. So he gave his allegiance where he could not give his esteem, and learned to respect sincerely the upright and moral character of one whom he yet regarded as an usurper. King William's government had little need to fear such a one. So he returned, as I have said, with a sobered heart and impoverished fortunes, to his ancestral house, which had fallen sadly to ruin while the owner had been a courtier, a soldier, and an exile. The roads into the Trough of Bolland were little more than cart-ruts; indeed, the way up to the house lay along a ploughed field before you came to the deer-park. Madam, as the country-folk used to call Mrs. Starkey, rode on a pillion behind her husband, holding on to him with a light hand by his leather riding-belt. Little master (he that was afterwards Squire Patrick Byrne Starkey) was held on to his pony by a serving-man. A woman past middle age walked, with a firm and strong step, by the cart that held much of the baggage; and high up on the mails and boxes, sat a girl of dazzling beauty, perched lightly on the topmost trunk, and swaying herself fearlessly to and fro, as the cart rocked and shook in the heavy roads of late autumn. The girl wore the Antwerp faille, or black Spanish mantle over her head, and altogether her appearance was such that the old cottager, who described the possession to me many years after, said that all the country-folk took her for a foreigner. Some dogs, and the boy who held them in charge, made up the company. They rode silently along, looking with grave, serious eyes at the people, who came out of the scattered cottages to bow or curtsy to the real Squire, "come back at last," and gazed after the little procession with gaping wonder, not deadened by the sound of the foreign language in which the few necessary words that passed among them were spoken. One lad, called from his staring by the Squire to come and help about the cart, accompanied them to the Manor-house. He said that when the lady had descended from her pillion, the middle-aged woman whom I have described as walking while the others rode, stepped quickly forward, and taking Madam Starkey (who was of a slight and delicate figure) in her arms, she lifted her over the threshold, and set her down in her husband's house, at the same time uttering a passionate and outlandish blessing. The Squire stood by, smiling gravely at first; but when the words of blessing were pronounced, he took off his fine feathered hat, and bent his head. The girl with the black mantle stepped onward into the shadow of the dark hall, and kissed the lady's hand; and that was all the lad could tell to the group that gathered round him on his return, eager to hear everything, and to know how much the Squire had given him for his services.

From all I could gather, the Manor-house, at the time of the Squire's return, was in the most dilapidated state. The stout gray walls remained firm and entire; but the inner chambers had been used for all kinds of purposes. The great withdrawing-room had been a barn; the state tapestry-chamber had held wool, and so on. But, by-and-by, they were cleared out; and if the Squire had no money to spend on new furniture, he and his wife had the knack of making the best of the old. He was no despicable joiner; she had a kind of grace in whatever she did, and imparted an air of elegant picturesqueness to whatever she touched. Besides, they had brought many rare things from the Continent; perhaps I should rather say, things that were rare in that part of England—carvings, and crosses, and beautiful pictures. And then, again, wood was plentiful in the Trough of Bolland, and great log-fires danced and glittered in all the dark, old rooms, and gave a look of home and comfort to everything.

Why do I tell you all this? I have little to do with the Squire and Madame Starkey; and yet I dwell upon them, as if I were unwilling to come to the real people with whom my life was so strangely mixed up. Madam had been nursed in Ireland by the very woman who lifted her in her arms, and welcomed her to her husband's home in Lancashire. Excepting for the short period of her own married life, Bridget Fitzgerald had never left her nursling. Her marriage—to one above her in rank—had been unhappy. Her husband had died, and left her in even greater poverty than that in which she was when he had first met with her. She had one child, the beautiful daughter who came riding on the waggon-load of furniture that was brought to the Manor-house. Madame Starkey had taken her again into her service when she became a widow. She and her daughter had followed "the mistress" in all her fortunes; they had lived at St. Germains and at Antwerp, and were now come to her home in Lancashire. As soon as Bridget had arrived there, the Squire gave her a cottage of her own, and took more pains in furnishing it for her than he did in anything else out of his own house. It was only nominally her residence. She was constantly up at the great house; indeed, it was but a short cut across the woods from her own home to the home of her nursling. Her daughter Mary, in like manner, moved from one house to the other at her own will. Madam loved both mother and child dearly. They had great influence over her, and, through her, over her husband. Whatever Bridget or Mary willed was sure to come to pass. They were not disliked; for, though wild and passionate, they were also generous by nature. But the other servants were afraid of them, as being in secret the ruling spirits of the household. The Squire had lost his interest in all secular things; Madam was gentle, affectionate, and yielding. Both husband and wife were tenderly attached to each other and to their boy; but they grew more and more to shun the trouble of decision on any point; and hence it was that Bridget could exert such despotic power. But if everyone else yielded to her "magic of a superior mind," her daughter not unfrequently rebelled. She and her mother were too much alike to agree. There were wild quarrels between them, and wilder reconciliations. There were times when, in the heat of passion, they could have stabbed each other. At all other times they both—Bridget especially—would have willingly laid down their lives for one another. Bridget's love for her child lay very deep—deeper than that daughter ever knew; or I should think she would never have wearied of home as she did, and prayed her mistress to obtain for her some situation—as waiting maid—beyond the seas, in that more cheerful continental life, among the scenes of which so many of her happiest years had been spent. She thought, as youth thinks, that life would last for ever, and that two or three years were but a small portion of it to pass away from her mother, whose only child she was. Bridget thought differently, but was too proud ever to show what she felt. If her child wished to leave her, why—she should go. But people said Bridget became ten years older in the course of two months at this time. She took it that Mary wanted to leave her. The truth was, that Mary wanted for a time to leave the place, and to seek some change, and would thankfully have taken her mother with her. Indeed when Madam Starkey had gotten her a situation with some grand lady abroad, and the time drew near for her to go, it was Mary who clung to her mother with passionate embrace, and, with floods of tears, declared that she would never leave her; and it was Bridget, who at last loosened her arms, and, grave and tearless herself, bade her keep her word, and go forth into the wide world. Sobbing aloud, and looking back continually, Mary went away. Bridget was still as death, scarcely drawing her breath, or closing her stony eyes; till at last she turned back into her cottage, and heaved a ponderous old settle against the door. There she sat, motionless, over the gray ashes of her extinguished fire, deaf to Madam's sweet voice, as she begged leave to enter and comfort her nurse. Deaf, stony, and motionless, she sat for more than twenty hours; till, for the third time, Madam came across the snowy path from the great house, carrying with her a young spaniel, which had been Mary's pet up at the hall; and which had not ceased all night long to seek for its absent mistress, and to whine and moan after her. With tears Madam told this story, through the closed door—tears excited by the terrible look of anguish, so steady, so immovable—so the same to-day as it was yesterday—on her nurse's face. The little creature in her arms began to utter its piteous cry, as it shivered with the cold. Bridget stirred; she moved—she listened. Again that long whine; she thought it was for her daughter; and what she had denied to her nursling and mistress she granted to the dumb creature that Mary had cherished. She opened the door, and took the dog from Madam's arms. Then Madam came in, and kissed and comforted the old woman, who took but little notice of her or anything. And sending up Master Patrick to the hall for fire and food, the sweet young lady never left her nurse all that night. Next day, the Squire himself came down, carrying a beautiful foreign picture—Our Lady of the Holy Heart, the Papists call it. It is a picture of the Virgin, her heart pierced with arrows, each arrow representing one of her great woes. That picture hung in Bridget's cottage when I first saw her; I have that picture now.

Years went on. Mary was still abroad. Bridget was still and stern, instead of active and passionate. The little dog, Mignon, was indeed her darling. I have heard that she talked to it continually; although, to most people, she was so silent. The Squire and Madam treated her with the greatest consideration, and well they might; for to them she was as devoted and faithful as ever. Mary wrote pretty often, and seemed satisfied with her life. But at length the letters ceased—I hardly know whether before or after a great and terrible sorrow came upon the house of the Starkeys. The Squire sickened of a putrid fever; and Madam caught it in nursing him, and died. You may be sure, Bridget let no other woman tend her but herself; and in the very arms that had received her at her birth, that sweet young woman laid her head down, and gave up her breath. The Squire recovered, in a fashion. He was never strong—he had never the heart to smile again. He fasted and prayed more than ever; and people did say that he tried to cut off the entail, and leave all the property away to found a monastery abroad, of which he prayed that some day little Squire Patrick might be the reverend father. But he could not do this, for the strictness of the entail and the laws against the Papists. So he could only appoint gentlemen of his own faith as guardians to his son, with many charges about the lad's soul, and a few about the land, and the way it was to be held while he was a minor. Of course, Bridget was not forgotten. He sent for her as he lay on his death-bed, and asked her if she would rather have a sum down, or have a small annuity settled upon her. She said at once she would have a sum down; for she thought of her daughter, and how she could bequeath the money to her, whereas an annuity would have died with her. So the Squire left her her cottage for life, and a fair sum of money. And then he died, with as ready and willing a heart as, I suppose, ever any gentleman took out of this world with him. The young Squire was carried off by his guardians, and Bridget was left alone.

I have said that she had not heard from Mary for some time. In her last letter, she had told of travelling about with her mistress, who was the English wife of some great foreign officer, and had spoken of her chances of making a good marriage, without naming the gentleman's name, keeping it rather back as a pleasant surprise to her mother; his station and fortune being, as I had afterwards reason to know, far superior to anything she had a right to expect. Then came a long silence; and Madam was dead, and the Squire was dead; and Bridget's heart was gnawed by anxiety, and she knew not whom to ask for news of her child. She could not write, and the Squire had managed her communication with her daughter. She walked off to Hurst; and got a good priest there—one whom she had known at Antwerp—to write for her. But no answer came. It was like crying into the' awful stillness of night.

One day, Bridget was missed by those neighbours who had been accustomed to mark her goings-out and comings-in. She had never been sociable with any of them; but the sight of her had become a part of their daily lives, and slow wonder arose in their minds, as morning after morning came, and her house-door remained closed, her window dead from any glitter, or light of fire within. At length, some one tried the door; it was locked. Two or three laid their heads together, before daring to look in through the blank unshuttered window. But, at last, they summoned up courage; and then saw that Bridget's absence from their little world was not the result of accident or death, but of premeditation. Such small articles of furniture as could be secured from the effects of time and damp by being packed up, were stowed away in boxes. The picture of the Madonna was taken down, and gone. In a word, Bridget had stolen away from her home, and left no trace whither she was departed. I knew afterwards, that she and her little dog had wandered off on the long search for her lost daughter. She was too illiterate to have faith in letters, even had she had the means of writing and sending many. But she had faith in her own strong love, and believed that her passionate instinct would guide her to her child. Besides, foreign travel was no new thing to her, and she could speak enough of French to explain the object of her journey, and had, moreover, the advantage of being, from her faith, a welcome object of charitable hospitality at many a distant convent. But the country people round Starkey Manor-house knew nothing of all this. They wondered what had become of her, in a torpid, lazy fashion, and then left off thinking of her altogether. Several years passed. Both Manor-house and cottage were deserted. The young Squire lived far away under the direction of his guardians. There were inroads of wool and corn into the sitting-rooms of the Hall; and there was some low talk, from time to time, among the hinds and country people whether it would not be as well to break into old Bridget's cottage, and save such of her goods as were left from the moth and rust which must be making sad havoc. But this idea was always quenched by the recollection of her strong character and passionate anger; and tales of her masterful spirit, and vehement force of will, were whispered about, till the very thought of offending her, by touching any article of hers, became invested with a kind of horror: it was believed that, dead or alive, she would not fail to avenge it. Suddenly she came home; with as little noise or note of preparation as she had departed. One day some one noticed a thin, blue curl of smoke ascending from her chimney. Her door stood open to the noonday sun; and, ere many hours had elapsed, some one had seen an old travel-and-sorrow-stained woman dipping her pitcher in the well; and said, that the dark, solemn eyes that looked up at him were more like Bridget Fitzgerald's than any one else's in this world; and yet, if it were she, she looked as if she had been scorched in the flames of hell, so brown, and scared, and fierce a creature did she seem. By- and-by many saw her; and those who met her eye once cared not to be caught looking at her again. She had got into the habit of perpetually talking to herself; nay, more, answering herself, and varying her tones according to the side she took at the moment. It was no wonder that those who dared to listen outside her door at night believed that she held converse with some spirit; in short, she was unconsciously earning for herself the dreadful reputation of a witch.

Her little dog, which had wandered half over the Continent with her, was her only companion; a dumb remembrancer of happier days. Once he was ill; and she carried him more than three miles, to ask about his management from one who had been groom to the last Squire, and had then been noted for his skill in all diseases of animals. Whatever this man did, the dog recovered; and they who heard her thanks, intermingled with blessings (that were rather promises of good fortune than prayers), looked grave at his good luck when, next year, his ewes twinned, and his meadow-grass was heavy and thick.

Now it so happened that, about the year seventeen hundred and eleven, one of the guardians of the young squire, a certain Sir Philip Tempest, bethought him of the good shooting there must be on his ward's property; and in consequence he brought down four or five gentlemen, of his friends, to stay for a week or two at the Hall. From all accounts, they roystered and spent pretty freely. I never heard any of their names but one, and that was Squire Gisborne's. He was hardly a middle-aged man then; he had been much abroad, and there, I believe, he had known Sir Philip Tempest, and done him some service. He was a daring and dissolute fellow in those days: careless and fearless, and one who would rather be in a quarrel than out of it. He had his fits of ill-temper besides, when he would spare neither man nor beast. Otherwise, those who knew him well, used to say he had a good heart, when he was neither drunk, nor angry, nor in any way vexed. He had altered much when I came to know him.

One day, the gentlemen had all been out shooting, and with but little success, I believe; anyhow, Mr. Gisborne had none, and was in a black humour accordingly. He was coming home, having his gun loaded, sportsman-like, when little Mignon crossed his path, just as he turned out of the wood by Bridget's cottage. Partly for wantonness, partly to vent his spleen upon some living creature. Mr. Gisborne took his gun, and fired—he had better have never fired gun again, than aimed that unlucky shot, he hit Mignon, and at the creature's sudden cry, Bridget came out, and saw at a glance what had been done. She took Mignon up in her arms, and looked hard at the wound; the poor dog looked at her with his glazing eyes, and tried to wag his tail and lick her hand, all covered with blood. Mr. Gisborne spoke in a kind of sullen penitence:

"You should have kept the dog out of my way—a little poaching varmint."
At this very moment, Mignon stretched out his legs, and stiffened in her arms—her lost Mary's dog, who had wandered and sorrowed with her for years. She walked right into Mr. Gisborne's path, and fixed his unwilling, sullen look, with her dark and terrible eye.
"Those never throve that did me harm," said she. "I'm alone in the world, and helpless; the more do the saints in heaven hear my prayers. Hear me, ye blessed ones! hear me while I ask for sorrow on this bad, cruel man. He has killed the only creature that loved me— the dumb beast that I loved. Bring down heavy sorrow on his head for it, O ye saints! He thought that I was helpless, because he saw me lonely and poor; but are not the armies of heaven for the like of me?"
"Come, come," said he, half remorseful, but not one whit afraid. "Here's a crown to buy thee another dog. Take it, and leave off cursing! I care none for thy threats."
"Don't you?" said she, coming a step closer, and changing her imprecatory cry for a whisper which made the gamekeeper's lad, following Mr. Gisborne, creep all over. "You shall live to see the creature you love best, and who alone loves you—ay, a human creature, but as innocent and fond as my poor, dead darling—you shall see this creature, for whom death would be too happy, become a terror and a loathing to all, for this blood's sake. Hear me, O holy saints, who never fail them that have no other help!"
She threw up her right hand, filled with poor Mignon's life-drops; they spirted, one or two of them, on his shooting-dress,—an ominous sight to the follower. But the master only laughed a little, forced, scornful laugh, and went on to the Hall. Before he got there, however, he took out a gold piece, and bade the boy carry it to the old woman on his return to the village. The lad was "afeared," as he told me in after years; he came to the cottage, and hovered about, not daring to enter. He peeped through the window at last; and by the flickering wood-flame, he saw Bridget kneeling before the picture of Our Lady of the Holy Heart, with dead Mignon lying between her and the Madonna. She was praying wildly, as her outstretched arms betokened. The lad shrunk away in redoubled terror; and contented himself with slipping the gold piece under the ill-fitting door. The next day it was thrown out upon the midden; and there it lay, no one daring to touch it.
Meanwhile Mr. Gisborne, half curious, half uneasy, thought to lessen his uncomfortable feelings by asking Sir Philip who Bridget was? He could only describe her—he did not know her name. Sir Philip was equally at a loss. But an old servant of the Starkeys, who had resumed his livery at the Hall on this occasion—a scoundrel whom Bridget had saved from dismissal more than once during her palmy days—said:-
"It will be the old witch, that his worship means. She needs a ducking, if ever a woman did, does that Bridget Fitzgerald."

"Fitzgerald!" said both the gentlemen at once. But Sir Philip was the first to continue:-
"I must have no talk of ducking her, Dickon. Why, she must be the very woman poor Starkey bade me have a care of; but when I came here last she was gone, no one knew where. I'll go and see her to-morrow. But mind you, sirrah, if any harm comes to her, or any more talk of her being a witch—I've a pack of hounds at home, who can follow the scent of a lying knave as well as ever they followed a dog-fox; so take care how you talk about ducking a faithful old servant of your dead master's."
"Had she ever a daughter?" asked Mr. Gisborne, after a while.
"I don't know—yes! I've a notion she had; a kind of waiting woman to Madam Starkey."
"Please your worship," said humbled Dickon, "Mistress Bridget had a daughter—one Mistress Mary—who went abroad, and has never been heard on since; and folk do say that has crazed her mother."
Mr. Gisborne shaded his eyes with his hand.
"I could wish she had not cursed me," he muttered. "She may have power—no one else could." After a while, he said aloud, no one understanding rightly what he meant, "Tush! it is impossible!"—and called for claret; and he and the other gentlemen set-to to a drinking-bout.

CHAPTER II.

I now come to the time in which I myself was mixed up with the people that I have been writing about. And to make you understand how I became connected with them, I must give you some little account of myself. My father was the younger son of a Devonshire gentleman of moderate property; my eldest uncle succeeded to the estate of his forefathers, my second became an eminent attorney in London, and my father took orders. Like most poor clergymen, he had a large family; and I have no doubt was glad enough when my London uncle, who was a bachelor, offered to take charge of me, and bring me up to be his successor in business.
In this way I came to live in London, in my uncle's house, not far from Gray's Inn, and to be treated and esteemed as his son, and to labour with him in his office. I was very fond of the old gentleman. He was the confidential agent of many country squires, and had attained to his present position as much by knowledge of human nature as by knowledge of law; though he was learned enough in the latter. He used to say his business was law, his pleasure heraldry. From his intimate acquaintance with family history, and all the tragic courses of life therein involved, to hear him talk, at leisure times, about any coat of arms that came across his path was as good as a play or a romance. Many cases of disputed property, dependent on a love of genealogy, were brought to him, as to a great authority on such

points. If the lawyer who came to consult him was young, he would take no fee, only give him a long lecture on the importance of attending to heraldry; if the lawyer was of mature age and good standing, he would mulct him pretty well, and abuse him to me afterwards as negligent of one great branch of the profession. His house was in a stately new street called Ormond Street, and in it he had a handsome library; but all the books treated of things that were past; none of them planned or looked forward into the future. I worked away—partly for the sake of my family at home, partly because my uncle had really taught me to enjoy the kind of practice in which he himself took such delight. I suspect I worked too hard; at any rate, in seventeen hundred and eighteen I was far from well, and my good uncle was disturbed by my ill looks.

One day, he rang the bell twice into the clerk's room at the dingy office in Grey's Inn Lane. It was the summons for me, and I went into his private room just as a gentleman—whom I knew well enough by sight as an Irish lawyer of more reputation than he deserved—was leaving.

My uncle was slowly rubbing his hands together and considering. I was there two or three minutes before he spoke. Then he told me that I must pack up my portmanteau that very afternoon, and start that night by posthorse for West Chester. I should get there, if all went well, at the end of five days' time, and must then wait for a packet to cross over to Dublin; from thence I must proceed to a certain town named Kildoon, and in that neighbourhood I was to remain, making certain inquiries as to the existence of any descendants of the younger branch of a family to whom some valuable estates had descended in the female line. The Irish lawyer whom I had seen was weary of the case, and would willingly have given up the property, without further ado, to a man who appeared to claim them; but on laying his tables and trees before my uncle, the latter had foreseen so many possible prior claimants, that the lawyer had begged him to undertake the management of the whole business. In his youth, my uncle would have liked nothing better than going over to Ireland himself, and ferreting out every scrap of paper or parchment, and every word of tradition respecting the family. As it was, old and gouty, he deputed me.

Accordingly, I went to Kildoon. I suspect I had something of my uncle's delight in following up a genealogical scent, for I very soon found out, when on the spot, that Mr. Rooney, the Irish lawyer, would have got both himself and the first claimant into a terrible scrape, if he had pronounced his opinion that the estates ought to be given up to him. There were three poor Irish fellows, each nearer of kin to the last possessor; but, a generation before, there was a still nearer relation, who had never been accounted for, nor his existence ever discovered by the lawyers, I venture to think, till I routed him out from the memory of some of the old dependants of the family. What had become of him? I travelled backwards and forwards; I crossed over to France, and came back again with a slight clue, which ended in my discovering that, wild and dissipated himself, he had left one child, a son, of yet worse character than his father; that this same Hugh Fitzgerald had married a very beautiful serving-woman of the Byrnes—a person below him in hereditary rank, but above him in character; that he had died soon after his marriage, leaving one child, whether a boy or a girl I could not learn, and that the mother had returned to live in the family of the Byrnes. Now, the chief of this latter family was serving in the Duke of Berwick's regiment, and it was long before I could hear from him; it was more than a year before I got a short, haughty letter—I fancy he had a soldier's contempt for a civilian, an Irishman's hatred for an Englishman, an exiled Jacobite's jealousy of one who prospered and lived tranquilly under the government he looked upon as an usurpation. "Bridget Fitzgerald," he said, "had been faithful to the fortunes of his sister—had followed her abroad, and to England when Mrs. Starkey had thought fit to return. Both his sister and her husband were dead, he knew nothing of Bridget Fitzgerald at the present time: probably Sir Philip Tempest, his nephew's guardian, might be able to give me some information." I have not given the little contemptuous terms; the way in which faithful service was meant to imply more than it said— all that has nothing to do with my story. Sir Philip, when applied to, told me that he paid an annuity regularly to an old woman named Fitzgerald, living at Coldholme (the village near Starkey Manor- house). Whether she had any descendants he could not say.

One bleak March evening, I came in sight of the places described at the beginning of my story. I could hardly understand the rude dialect in which the direction to old Bridget's house was given.

"Yo' see yon furleets," all run together, gave me no idea that I was to guide myself by the distant lights that shone in the windows of the Hall, occupied for the time by a farmer who held the post of steward, while the Squire, now four or five and twenty, was making the grand tour. However, at last, I reached Bridget's cottage—a low, moss-grown place: the palings that had once surrounded it were broken and gone; and the underwood of the forest came up to the walls, and must have darkened the windows. It was about seven o'clock—not late to my London notions—but, after knocking for some time at the door and receiving no reply, I was driven to conjecture that the occupant of the house was gone to bed. So I betook myself to the nearest church I had seen, three miles back on the road I had come, sure that close to that I should find an inn of some kind; and early the next morning I set off back to Coldholme, by a field-path which my host assured me I should find a shorter cut than the road I had taken the night before. It was a cold, sharp morning; my feet left prints in the sprinkling of hoar-frost that covered the ground; nevertheless, I saw an old woman, whom I instinctively suspected to be the object of my search, in a sheltered covert

on one side of my path. I lingered and watched her. She must have been considerably above the middle size in her prime, for when she raised herself from the stooping position in which I first saw her, there was something fine and commanding in the erectness of her figure. She drooped again in a minute or two, and seemed looking for something on the ground, as, with bent head, she turned off from the spot where I gazed upon her, and was lost to my sight. I fancy I missed my way, and made a round in spite of the landlord's directions; for by the time I had reached Bridget's cottage she was there, with no semblance of hurried walk or discomposure of any kind. The door was slightly ajar. I knocked, and the majestic figure stood before me, silently awaiting the explanation of my errand. Her teeth were all gone, so the nose and chin were brought near together; the gray eyebrows were straight, and almost hung over her deep, cavernous eyes, and the thick white hair lay in silvery masses over the low, wide, wrinkled forehead. For a moment, I stood uncertain how to shape my answer to the solemn questioning of her silence.
"Your name is Bridget Fitzgerald, I believe?"
She bowed her head in assent.
"I have something to say to you. May I come in? I am unwilling to keep you standing."
"You cannot tire me," she said, and at first she seemed inclined to deny me the shelter of her roof. But the next moment—she had searched the very soul in me with her eyes during that instant—she led me in, and dropped the shadowing hood of her gray, draping cloak, which had previously hid part of the character of her countenance. The cottage was rude and bare enough. But before the picture of the Virgin, of which I have made mention, there stood a little cup filled with fresh primroses. While she paid her reverence to the Madonna, I understood why she had been out seeking through the clumps of green in the sheltered copse. Then she turned round, and bade me be seated. The expression of her face, which all this time I was studying, was not bad, as the stories of my last night's landlord had led me to expect; it was a wild, stern, fierce, indomitable countenance, seamed and scarred by agonies of solitary weeping; but it was neither cunning nor malignant.
"My name is Bridget Fitzgerald," said she, by way of opening our conversation.
"And your husband was Hugh Fitzgerald, of Knock Mahon, near Kildoon, in Ireland?"
A faint light came into the dark gloom of her eyes.
"He was."
"May I ask if you had any children by him?"
The light in her eyes grew quick and red. She tried to speak, I could see; but something rose in her throat, and choked her, and until she could speak

calmly, she would fain not speak at all before a stranger. In a minute or so she said—"I had a daughter—one Mary Fitzgerald,"—then her strong nature mastered her strong will, and she cried out, with a trembling wailing cry: "Oh, man! what of her?--what of her?"

She rose from her seat, and came and clutched at my arm, and looked in my eyes. There she read, as I suppose, my utter ignorance of what had become of her child; for she went blindly back to her chair, and sat rocking herself and softly moaning, as if I were not there; I not daring to speak to the lone and awful woman. After a little pause, she knelt down before the picture of Our Lady of the Holy Heart, and spoke to her by all the fanciful and poetic names of the Litany.

"O Rose of Sharon! O Tower of David! O Star of the Sea! have ye no comfort for my sore heart? Am I for ever to hope? Grant me at least despair!"—and so on she went, heedless of my presence. Her prayers grew wilder and wilder, till they seemed to me to touch on the borders of madness and blasphemy. Almost involuntarily, I spoke as if to stop her.

"Have you any reason to think that your daughter is dead?

She rose from her knees, and came and stood before me.

"Mary Fitzgerald is dead," said she. "I shall never see her again in the flesh. No tongue ever told me; but I know she is dead. I have yearned so to see her, and my heart's will is fearful and strong: it would have drawn her to me before now, if she had been a wanderer on the other side of the world. I wonder often it has not drawn her out of the grave to come and stand before me, and hear me tell her how I loved her. For, sir, we parted unfriends."

I knew nothing but the dry particulars needed for my lawyer's quest, but I could not help feeling for the desolate woman; and she must have read the unusual sympathy with her wistful eyes.

"Yes, sir, we did. She never knew how I loved her; and we parted unfriends; and I fear me that I wished her voyage might not turn out well, only meaning,—O, blessed Virgin! you know I only meant that she should come home to her mother's arms as to the happiest place on earth; but my wishes are terrible—their power goes beyond my thought—and there is no hope for me, if my words brought Mary harm."

"But," I said, "you do not know that she is dead. Even now, you hoped she might be alive. Listen to me," and I told her the tale I have already told you, giving it all in the driest manner, for I wanted to recall the clear sense that I felt almost sure she had possessed in her younger days, and by keeping up her attention to details, restrain the vague wildness of her grief.

She listened with deep attention, putting from time to time such questions as convinced me I had to do with no common intelligence, however dimmed and shorn by solitude and mysterious sorrow. Then she took up her tale; and in few brief words, told me of her wanderings abroad in vain search after her daughter; sometimes in the wake of armies, sometimes in camp, sometimes in city. The lady, whose waiting-woman Mary had gone to be, had died soon after the date of her last letter home; her husband, the foreign officer, had been serving in Hungary, whither Bridget had followed him, but too late to find him. Vague rumours reached her that Mary had made a great marriage: and this sting of doubt was added,—whether the mother might not be close to her child under her new name, and even hearing of her every day; and yet never recognizing the lost one under the appellation she then bore. At length the thought took possession of her, that it was possible that all this time Mary might be at home at Coldholme, in the Trough of Bolland, in Lancashire, in England; and home came Bridget, in that vain hope, to her desolate hearth, and empty cottage. Here she had thought it safest to remain; if Mary was in life, it was here she would seek for her mother.

I noted down one or two particulars out of Bridget's narrative that I thought might be of use to me: for I was stimulated to further search in a strange and extraordinary manner. It seemed as if it were impressed upon me, that I must take up the quest where Bridget had laid it down; and this for no reason that had previously influenced me (such as my uncle's anxiety on the subject, my own reputation as a lawyer, and so on), but from some strange power which had taken possession of my will only that very morning, and which forced it in the direction it chose.

"I will go," said I. "I will spare nothing in the search. Trust to me. I will learn all that can be learnt. You shall know all that money, or pains, or wit can discover. It is true she may be long dead: but she may have left a child."

"A child!" she cried, as if for the first time this idea had struck her mind. "Hear him, Blessed Virgin! he says she may have left a child. And you have never told me, though I have prayed so for a sign, waking or sleeping!"

"Nay," said I, "I know nothing but what you tell me. You say you heard of her marriage."

But she caught nothing of what I said. She was praying to the Virgin in a kind of ecstasy, which seemed to render her unconscious of my very presence.

From Coldholme I went to Sir Philip Tempest's. The wife of the foreign officer had been a cousin of his father's, and from him I thought I might gain some particulars as to the existence of the Count de la Tour d'Auvergne, and where I could find him; for I knew questions de vive voix aid the flagging recollection, and I was determined to lose no chance for want of trouble. But Sir Philip had gone abroad, and it would be some time before I could receive an answer. So I followed my uncle's advice, to whom I had mentioned how wearied I felt, both in body and mind, by my will-o'-the-wisp search. He immediately told me to go to Harrogate, there to await Sir Philip's reply. I should be near to one of the places connected with my search, Coldholme; not far from Sir Philip Tempest, in case he returned, and I wished to ask him any further questions; and, in conclusion, my uncle bade me try to forget all about my business for a time.

This was far easier said than done. I have seen a child on a common blown along by a high wind, without power of standing still and resisting the tempestuous force. I was somewhat in the same predicament as regarded my mental state. Something resistless seemed to urge my thoughts on, through every possible course by which there was a chance of attaining to my object. I did not see the sweeping moors when I walked out: when I held a book in my hand, and read the words, their sense did not penetrate to my brain. If I slept, I went on with the same ideas, always flowing in the same direction. This could not last long without having a bad effect on the body. I had an illness, which, although I was racked with pain, was a positive relief to me, as it compelled me to live in the present suffering, and not in the visionary researches I had been continually making before. My kind uncle came to nurse me; and after the immediate danger was over, my life seemed to slip away in delicious languor for two or three months. I did not ask—so much did I dread falling into the old channel of thought—whether any reply had been received to my letter to Sir Philip. I turned my whole imagination right away from all that subject. My uncle remained with me until nigh midsummer, and then returned to his business in London; leaving me perfectly well, although not completely strong. I was to follow him in a fortnight; when, as he said, "we would look over letters, and talk about several things." I knew what this little speech alluded to, and shrank from the train of thought it suggested, which was so intimately connected with my first feelings of illness. However, I had a fortnight more to roam on those invigorating Yorkshire moors.

In those days, there was one large, rambling inn, at Harrogate, close to the Medicinal Spring; but it was already becoming too small for the accommodation of the influx of visitors, and many lodged round about, in the farm-houses of the district. It was so early in the season, that I had the inn pretty much to myself; and, indeed, felt rather like a visitor in a private house, so intimate had the landlord and landlady become with me during my long illness. She would chide me for being out so late on the moors, or for having been too long without food, quite in a motherly way; while he consulted me about vintages and wines, and taught me many a Yorkshire wrinkle about horses. In my walks I met other strangers from time to time. Even before my uncle had left me, I had noticed, with half-torpid curiosity, a young lady of very striking appearance, who went about always accompanied by an elderly companion,—hardly a gentlewoman, but with something in her look that prepossessed me in her favour. The younger lady always put her veil down when any one approached; so it had been only once or twice, when I had come upon her at a sudden turn in the path, that I had even had a glimpse at her face. I am not sure if it was beautiful, though in after-life I grew to think it so. But it was at this time overshadowed by a sadness that never varied: a pale, quiet, resigned look of intense suffering, that irresistibly attracted me,—not with love, but with a sense of infinite compassion for one so young yet so hopelessly unhappy. The companion wore something of the same look: quiet melancholy, hopeless, yet resigned. I asked my landlord who they were. He said they were called Clarke, and wished to be considered as mother and daughter; but that, for his part, he did not believe that to be their right name, or that there was any such relationship between them. They had been in the neighbourhood of Harrogate for some time, lodging in a remote farm-house. The people there would tell nothing about them; saying that they paid handsomely, and never did any harm; so why should they be speaking of any strange things that might happen? That, as the landlord shrewdly observed, showed there was something out of the common way he had heard that the elderly woman was a cousin of the farmer's where they lodged, and so the regard existing between relations might help to keep them quiet.

"What did he think, then, was the reason for their extreme seclusion?" asked I.

"Nay, he could not tell,—not he. He had heard that the young lady, for all as quiet as she seemed, played strange pranks at times." He shook his head when I asked him for more particulars, and refused to give them, which made me doubt if he knew any, for he was in general a talkative and communicative man. In default of other interests, after my uncle left, I set myself to watch these two people. I hovered about their walks drawn towards them with a strange fascination, which was not diminished by their evident annoyance at so frequently meeting me. One day, I had the sudden good fortune to be at hand when they were alarmed by the attack of a bull, which, in those unenclosed grazing districts, was a particularly dangerous occurrence. I have other and more important things to relate, than to tell of the accident which gave me an opportunity of rescuing them, it is enough to say, that this event was the beginning of an acquaintance, reluctantly acquiesced in by them, but eagerly prosecuted by me. I can hardly tell when intense curiosity became merged in love, but in less than ten days after my uncle's departure I was passionately enamoured of Mistress Lucy, as her attendant called her; carefully—for this I noted well—avoiding any address which appeared as if there was an equality of station between them. I noticed also that Mrs. Clarke, the elderly woman, after her first reluctance to allow me to pay them any attentions had been overcome, was cheered by my evident attachment to the young girl; it seemed to lighten her heavy burden of care, and she evidently favoured my visits to the farmhouse where they lodged. It was not so with Lucy. A more attractive person I never saw, in spite of her depression of manner, and shrinking avoidance of me. I felt sure at once, that whatever was the source of her grief, it rose from no fault of her own. It was difficult to draw her into conversation; but when at times, for a moment or two, I beguiled her into talk, I could see a rare intelligence in her face, and a grave, trusting look in the soft, gray eyes that were raised for a minute to mine. I made every excuse I possibly could for going there. I sought wild flowers for Lucy's sake; I planned walks for Lucy's sake; I watched the heavens by night, in hopes that some unusual beauty of sky would justify me in tempting Mrs. Clarke and Lucy forth upon the moors, to gaze at the great purple dome above.

It seemed to me that Lucy was aware of my love; but that, for some motive which I could not guess, she would fain have repelled me; but then again I saw, or fancied I saw, that her heart spoke in my favour, and that there was a struggle going on in her mind, which at times (I loved so dearly) I could have begged her to spare herself, even though the happiness of my whole life should have been the sacrifice; for her complexion grew paler, her aspect of sorrow more hopeless, her delicate frame yet slighter. During this period I had written, I should say, to my uncle, to beg to be allowed to prolong my stay at Harrogate, not giving any reason; but such was his tenderness towards me, that in a few days I heard from him, giving me a willing permission, and only charging me to take care of myself, and not use too much exertion during the hot weather.

One sultry evening I drew near the farm. The windows of their parlour were open, and I heard voices when I turned the corner of the house, as I passed the first window (there were two windows in their little ground-floor room). I saw Lucy distinctly; but when I had knocked at their door—the house-door stood always ajar—she was gone, and I saw only Mrs. Clarke, turning over the work-things lying on the table, in a nervous and purposeless manner. I felt by instinct that a conversation of some importance was coming on, in which I should be expected to say what was my object in paying these frequent visits. I was glad of the opportunity. My uncle had several times alluded to the pleasant possibility of my bringing home a young wife, to cheer and adorn the old house in Ormond Street. He was rich, and I was to succeed him, and had, as I knew, a fair reputation for so young a lawyer. So on my side I saw no obstacle. It was true that Lucy was shrouded in mystery; her name (I was convinced it was not Clarke), birth, parentage, and previous life were unknown to me. But I was sure of her goodness and sweet innocence, and although I knew that there must be something painful to be told, to account for her mournful sadness, yet I was willing to bear my share in her grief, whatever it might be.

Mrs. Clarke began, as if it was a relief to her to plunge into the subject.

"We have thought, sir—at least I have thought—that you knew very little of us, nor we of you, indeed; not enough to warrant the intimate acquaintance we have fallen into. I beg your pardon, sir," she went on, nervously; "I am but a plain kind of woman, and I mean to use no rudeness; but I must say straight out that I—we—think it would be better for you not to come so often to see us. She is very unprotected, and—"

"Why should I not come to see you, dear madam?" asked I, eagerly, glad of the opportunity of explaining myself. "I come, I own, because I have learnt to love Mistress Lucy, and wish to teach her to love me.

Mistress Clarke shook her head, and sighed.

"Don't, sir—neither love her, nor, for the sake of all you hold sacred, teach her to love you! If I am too late, and you love her already, forget her,—forget these last few weeks. O! I should never have allowed you to come!" she went on passionately; "but what am I to do? We are forsaken by all, except the great God, and even He permits a strange and evil power to afflict us—what am I to do! Where is it to end?" She wrung her hands in her distress; then she turned to me: "Go away, sir! go away, before you learn to care any more for her. I ask it for your own sake—I implore! You have been good and kind to us, and we shall always recollect you with gratitude; but go away now, and never come back to cross our fatal path!"

"Indeed, madam," said I, "I shall do no such thing. You urge it for my own sake. I have no fear, so urged—nor wish, except to hear more—all. I cannot have seen Mistress Lucy in all the intimacy of this last fortnight, without acknowledging her goodness and innocence; and without seeing—pardon me, madam—that for some reason you are two very lonely women, in some mysterious sorrow and distress. Now, though I am not powerful myself, yet I have friends who are so wise and kind that they may be said to possess power. Tell me some particulars. Why are you in grief—what is your secret- -why are you here? I declare solemnly that nothing you have said has daunted me in my wish to become Lucy's husband; nor will I shrink from any difficulty that, as such an aspirant, I may have to encounter. You say you are friendless—why cast away an honest friend? I will tell you of people to whom you may write, and who will answer any questions as to my character and prospects. I do not shun inquiry."

She shook her head again. "You had better go away, sir. You know nothing about us."

"I know your names," said I, "and I have heard you allude to the part of the country from which you came, which I happen to know as a wild and lonely place. There are so few people living in it that, if I chose to go there, I could easily ascertain all about you; but I would rather hear it from yourself." You see I wanted to pique her into telling me something definite.

"You do not know our true names, sir," said she, hastily.

"Well, I may have conjectured as much. But tell me, then, I conjure you. Give me your reasons for distrusting my willingness to stand by what I have said with regard to Mistress Lucy."

"Oh, what can I do?" exclaimed she. "If I am turning away a true friend, as he says?—Stay!" coming to a sudden decision—" I will tell you something—I cannot tell you all—you would not believe it. But, perhaps, I can tell you enough to prevent your going on in your hopeless attachment. I am not Lucy's mother."

"So I conjectured," I said. "Go on."

"I do not even know whether she is the legitimate or illegitimate child of her father. But he is cruelly turned against her; and her mother is long dead; and for a terrible reason, she has no other creature to keep constant to her but me. She—only two years ago— such a darling and such a pride in her father's house! Why, sir, there is a mystery that might happen in connection with her any moment; and then you would go away like all the rest; and, when you next heard her name, you would loathe her. Others, who have loved her longer, have done so before now. My poor child! whom neither God nor man has mercy upon—or, surely, she would die!"

The good woman was stopped by her crying. I confess, I was a little stunned by her last words; but only for a moment. At any rate, till I knew definitely what was this mysterious stain upon one so simple and pure, as Lucy seemed, I would not desert her, and so I said; and she made me answer:-

"If you are daring in your heart to think harm of my child, sir, after knowing her as you have done, you are no good man yourself; but I am so foolish and helpless in my great sorrow, that I would fain hope to find a friend in you. I cannot help trusting that, although you may no longer feel toward her as a lover, you will have pity upon us; and perhaps, by your learning you can tell us where to go for aid."

"I implore you to tell me what this mystery is," I cried, almost maddened by this suspense.

"I cannot," said she, solemnly. "I am under a deep vow of secrecy. If you are to be told, it must be by her." She left the room, and I remained to ponder over this strange interview. I mechanically turned over the few books, and with eyes that saw nothing at the time, examined the tokens of Lucy's frequent presence in that room.

When I got home at night, I remembered how all these trifles spoke of a pure and tender heart and innocent life. Mistress Clarke returned; she had been crying sadly.

"Yes," said she, "it is as I feared: she loves you so much that she is willing to run the fearful risk of telling you all herself—she acknowledges it is but a poor chance; but your sympathy will be a balm, if you give it. To-morrow, come here at ten in the morning; and, as you hope for pity in your hour of agony, repress all show of fear or repugnance you may feel towards one so grievously afflicted."

I half smiled. "Have no fear," I said. It seemed too absurd to imagine my feeling dislike to Lucy.

"Her father loved her well," said she, gravely, "yet he drove her out like some monstrous thing."

Just at this moment came a peal of ringing laughter from the garden. It was Lucy's voice; it sounded as if she were standing just on one side of the open casement—and as though she were suddenly stirred to merriment—merriment verging on boisterousness, by the doings or sayings of some other person. I can scarcely say why, but the sound jarred on me inexpressibly. She knew the subject of our conversation, and must have been at least aware of the state of agitation her friend was in; she herself usually so gentle and quiet. I half rose to go to the window, and satisfy my instinctive curiosity as to what had provoked this burst of, ill-timed laughter; but Mrs. Clarke threw her whole weight and power upon the hand with which she pressed and kept me down.

"For God's sake!" she said, white and trembling all over, "sit still; be quiet. Oh! be patient. To-morrow you will know all. Leave us, for we are all sorely afflicted. Do not seek to know more about us."

Again that laugh—so musical in sound, yet so discordant to my heart. She held me tight—tighter; without positive violence I could not have risen. I was sitting with my back to the window, but I felt a shadow pass between the sun's warmth and me, and a strange shudder ran through my frame. In a minute or two she released me.

"Go," repeated she. "Be warned, I ask you once more. I do not think you can stand this knowledge that you seek. If I had had my own way, Lucy should never have yielded, and promised to tell you all. Who knows what may come of it?"

"I am firm in my wish to know all. I return at ten tomorrow morning, and then expect to see Mistress Lucy herself."

I turned away; having my own suspicions, I confess, as to Mistress Clarke's sanity.

Conjectures as to the meaning of her hints, and uncomfortable thoughts connected with that strange laughter, filled my mind. I could hardly sleep. I rose early; and long before the hour I had appointed, I was on the path over the common that led to the old farm-house where they lodged. I suppose that Lucy had passed no better a night than I; for there she was also, slowly pacing with her even step, her eyes bent down, her whole look most saintly and pure. She started when I came close to her, and grew paler as I reminded her of my appointment, and spoke with something of the impatience of obstacles that, seeing her once more, had called up afresh in my mind. All strange and terrible hints, and giddy merriment were forgotten. My heart gave forth words of fire, and my tongue uttered them. Her colour went and came, as she listened; but, when I had ended my passionate speeches, she lifted her soft eyes to me, and said -

"But you know that you have something to learn about me yet. I only want to say this: I shall not think less of you—less well of you, I mean—if you, too, fall away from me when you know all. Stop!" said she, as if fearing another burst of mad words. "Listen to me. My father is a man of great wealth. I never knew my mother; she must have died when I was very young. When first I remember anything, I was living in a great, lonely house, with my dear and faithful Mistress Clarke. My father, even, was not there; he was—he is—a soldier, and his duties lie aboard. But he came from time to time, and every time I think he loved me more and more. He brought me rarities from foreign lands, which prove to me now how much he must have thought of me during his absences. I can sit down and measure the depth of his lost love now, by such standards as these. I never thought whether he loved me or not, then; it was so natural, that it was like the air I breathed. Yet he was an angry man at times, even then; but never with me. He was very reckless, too; and, once or twice, I heard a whisper among the servants that a doom was over him, and that he knew it, and tried to drown his knowledge in wild activity, and even sometimes, sir, in wine. So I grew up in this grand mansion, in that lonely place. Everything around me seemed at my disposal, and I think every one loved me; I am sure I loved them. Till about two years ago—I remember it well—my father had come to England, to us; and he seemed so proud and so pleased with me and all I had done. And one day his tongue seemed loosened with wine, and he told me much that I had not known till then,—how dearly he had loved my mother, yet how his wilful usage had caused her death; and then he went on to say how he loved me better than any creature on earth, and how, some day, he hoped to take me to foreign places, for that he could hardly bear these long absences from his only child. Then he seemed to change suddenly, and said, in a strange, wild way, that I was not to believe what he said; that there was many a thing he loved better—his horse—his dog—I know not what.

"And 'twas only the next morning that, when I came into his room to ask his blessing as was my wont, he received me with fierce and angry words. 'Why had I,' so he asked, 'been delighting myself in such wanton mischief—dancing over the tender plants in the flower-beds, all set with the famous Dutch bulbs he had brought from Holland?' I had never been out of doors that morning, sir, and I could not conceive what he meant, and so I said; and then he swore at me for a liar, and said I was of no true blood, for he had seen me doing all that mischief himself—with his own eyes. What could I say? He would not listen to me, and even my tears seemed only to irritate him. That day was the beginning of my great sorrows. Not long after, he reproached me for my undue familiarity—all unbecoming a gentlewoman—with his grooms. I had been in the stable-yard, laughing and talking, he said. Now, sir, I am something of a coward by nature, and I had always dreaded horses; be-sides that, my father's servants—those whom he brought with him from foreign parts- -were wild fellows, whom I had always avoided, and to whom I had never spoken, except as a lady must needs from time to time speak to her father's people. Yet my father called me by names of which I hardly know the meaning, but my heart told me they were such as shame any modest woman; and from that day he turned quite against me;—nay, sir, not many weeks after that, he came in with a riding-whip in his hand; and, accusing me harshly of evil doings, of which I knew no more than you, sir, he was about to strike me, and I, all in bewildering tears, was ready to take his stripes as great kindness compared to his harder words, when suddenly he stopped his arm mid- way, gasped and staggered, crying out, 'The curse—the curse!' I looked up in terror. In the great mirror opposite I saw myself, and right behind, another wicked, fearful self, so like me that my soul seemed to quiver within me, as though not knowing to which similitude of body it belonged. My father saw my double at the same moment, either in its dreadful reality, whatever that might be, or in the scarcely less terrible reflection in the mirror; but what came of it at that moment I cannot say, for I suddenly swooned away; and when I came to myself I was lying in my bed, and my faithful Clarke sitting by me. I was in my bed for days; and even while I lay there my double was seen by all, flitting about the house and gardens, always about some mischievous or detestable work. What wonder that every one shrank from me in dread—that my father drove me forth at length, when the disgrace of which I was the cause was past his patience to bear. Mistress Clarke came with me; and here we try to live such a life of piety and prayer as may in time set me free from the curse."

All the time she had been speaking, I had been weighing her story in my mind. I had hitherto put cases of witchcraft on one side, as mere superstitions; and my uncle and I had had many an argument, he supporting himself by the opinion of his good friend Sir Matthew Hale. Yet this sounded like the tale of one bewitched; or was it merely the effect of a life of extreme seclusion telling on the nerves of a sensitive girl? My scepticism inclined me to the latter belief, and when she paused I said:

"I fancy that some physician could have disabused your father of his belief in visions—"

Just at that instant, standing as I was opposite to her in the full and perfect morning light, I saw behind her another figure—a ghastly resemblance, complete in likeness, so far as form and feature and minutest touch of dress could go, but with a loathsome demon soul looking out of the gray eyes, that were in turns mocking and voluptuous. My heart stood still within me; every hair rose up erect; my flesh crept with horror. I could not see the grave and tender Lucy—my eyes were fascinated by the creature beyond. I know not why, but I put out my hand to clutch it; I grasped nothing but empty air, and my whole blood curdled to ice. For a moment I could not see; then my sight came back, and I saw Lucy standing before me, alone, deathly pale, and, I could have fancied, almost, shrunk in size.

"IT has been near me?" she said, as if asking a question.

The sound seemed taken out of her voice; it was husky as the notes on an old harpsichord when the strings have ceased to vibrate. She read her answer in my face, I suppose, for I could not speak. Her look was one of intense fear, but that died away into an aspect of most humble patience. At length she seemed to force herself to face behind and around her: she saw the purple moors, the blue distant hills, quivering in the sunlight, but nothing else.

"Will you take me home?" she said, meekly.

I took her by the hand, and led her silently through the budding heather—we dared not speak; for we could not tell but that the dread creature was listening, although unseen,—but that IT might appear and push us asunder. I never loved her more fondly than now when— and that was the unspeakable misery—the idea of her was becoming so inextricably blended with the shuddering thought of IT. She seemed to understand what I must be feeling. She let go my hand, which she had kept clasped until then, when we reached the garden gate, and went forwards to meet her anxious friend, who was standing by the window looking for her. I could not enter the house: I needed silence, society, leisure, change—I knew not what—to shake off the sensation of that creature's presence. Yet I lingered about the garden—I hardly know why; I partly suppose, because I feared to encounter the resemblance again on the solitary common, where it had vanished, and partly from a feeling of inexpressible compassion for Lucy. In a few minutes Mistress Clarke came forth and joined me. We walked some paces in silence.

"You know all now," said she, solemnly.

"I saw IT," said I, below my breath.

"And you shrink from us, now," she said, with a hopelessness which stirred up all that was brave or good in me.

"Not a whit," said I. "Human flesh shrinks from encounter with the powers of darkness: and, for some reason unknown to me, the pure and holy Lucy is their victim."

"The sins of the fathers shall be visited upon the children," she said.

"Who is her father?" asked I. "Knowing as much as I do, I may surely know more—know all. Tell me, I entreat you, madam, all that you can conjecture respecting this demoniac persecution of one so good."

"I will; but not now. I must go to Lucy now. Come this afternoon, I will see you alone; and oh, sir! I will trust that you may yet find some way to help us in our sore trouble!"

I was miserably exhausted by the swooning affright which had taken possession of me. When I reached the inn, I staggered in like one overcome by wine. I went to my own private room. It was some time before I saw that the weekly post had come in, and brought me my letters. There was one from my uncle, one from my home in Devonshire, and one, re-directed over the first address, sealed with a great coat of arms, It was from Sir Philip Tempest: my letter of inquiry respecting Mary Fitzgerald had reached him at Liege, where it so happened that the Count de la Tour d'Auvergne was quartered at the very time. He remembered his wife's beautiful attendant; she had had high words with the deceased countess, respecting her intercourse with an English gentleman of good standing, who was also in the foreign service. The countess augured evil of his intentions; while Mary, proud and vehement, asserted that he would soon marry her, and resented her mistress's warnings as an insult. The consequence was, that she had left Madame de la Tour d'Auvergne's service, and, as the Count believed, had gone to live with the Englishman; whether he had married her, or not, he could not say. "But," added Sir Philip Tempest, you may easily hear what particulars you wish to know respecting Mary Fitzgerald from the Englishman himself, if, as I suspect, he is no other than my neighbour and former acquaintance, Mr. Gisborne, of Skipford Hall, in the West Riding. I am led to the belief that he is no other, by several small particulars, none of which are in themselves conclusive, but which, taken together, furnish a mass of presumptive evidence. As far as I could make out from the Count's foreign pronunciation, Gisborne was the name of the Englishman: I know that Gisborne of Skipford was abroad and in the foreign service at that time—he was a likely fellow enough for such an exploit, and, above all, certain expressions recur to my mind which he used in reference to old Bridget Fitzgerald, of Coldholme, whom he once encountered while staying with me at Starkey Manor-house. I remember that the meeting seemed to have produced some extraordinary effect upon his mind, as though he had suddenly discovered some connection which she might have had with his previous life. I beg you to let me know if I can be of any further service to you. Your uncle once rendered me a good turn, and I will gladly repay it, so far as in me lies, to his nephew."

I was now apparently close on the discovery which I had striven so many months to attain. But success had lost its zest. I put my letters down, and seemed to forget them all in thinking of the morning I had passed that very day. Nothing was real but the unreal presence, which had come like an evil blast across my bodily eyes, and burnt itself down upon my brain. Dinner came, and went away untouched. Early in the afternoon I walked to the farm-house. I found Mistress Clarke alone, and I was glad and relieved. She was evidently prepared to tell me all I might wish to hear.

"You asked me for Mistress Lucy's true name; it is Gisborne," she began.

"Not Gisborne of Skipford?" I exclaimed, breathless with anticipation.

"The same," said she, quietly, not regarding my manner. "Her father is a man of note; although, being a Roman Catholic, he cannot take that rank in this country to which his station entitles him. The consequence is that he lives much abroad—has been a soldier, I am told."

"And Lucy's mother?" I asked.

She shook her head. "I never knew her," said she. "Lucy was about three years old when I was engaged to take charge of her. Her mother was dead."

"But you know her name?—you can tell if it was Mary Fitzgerald?"

She looked astonished. "That was her name. But, sir, how came you to be so well acquainted with it? It was a mystery to the whole household at Skipford Court. She was some beautiful young woman whom he lured away from her protectors while he was abroad. I have heard said he practised some terrible deceit upon her, and when she came to know it, she was neither to have nor to hold, but rushed off from his very arms, and threw herself into a rapid stream and was drowned. It stung him deep with remorse, but I used to think the remembrance of the mother's cruel death made him love the child yet dearer."

I told her, as briefly as might be, of my researches after the descendant and heir of the Fitzgeralds of Kildoon, and added— something of my old lawyer spirit returning into me for the moment— that I had no doubt but that we should prove Lucy to be by right possessed of large estates in Ireland.

No flush came over her gray face; no light into her eyes. "And what is all the wealth in the whole world to that poor girl?" she said. "It will not free her from the ghastly bewitchment which persecutes her. As for money, what a pitiful thing it is! it cannot touch her."

"No more can the Evil Creature harm her," I said. "Her holy nature dwells apart, and cannot be defiled or stained by all the devilish arts in the whole world."

"True! but it is a cruel fate to know that all shrink from her, sooner or later, as from one possessed—accursed."

"How came it to pass?" I asked.

"Nay, I know not. Old rumours there are, that were bruited through the household at Skipford."

"Tell me," I demanded.

"They came from servants, who would fain account for every thing. They say that, many years ago, Mr. Gisborne killed a dog belonging to an old witch at Coldholme; that she cursed, with a dreadful and mysterious curse, the creature, whatever it might be, that he should love best; and that it struck so deeply into his heart that for years he kept himself aloof from any temptation to love aught. But who could help loving Lucy?"

"You never heard the witch's name?" I gasped.

"Yes—they called her Bridget: they said he would never go near the spot again for terror of her. Yet he was a brave man!"

"Listen," said I, taking hold of her arm, the better to arrest her full attention: "if what I suspect holds true, that man stole Bridget's only child—the very Mary Fitzgerald who was Lucy's mother; if so, Bridget cursed him in ignorance of the deeper wrong he had done her. To this hour she yearns after her lost child, and questions the saints whether she be living or not. The roots of that curse lie deeper than she knows: she unwittingly banned him for a deeper guilt than that of killing a dumb beast. The sins of the fathers are indeed visited upon the children."

"But," said Mistress Clarke, eagerly, "she would never let evil rest on her own grandchild? Surely, sir, if what you say be true, there are hopes for Lucy. Let us go—go at once, and tell this fearful woman all that you suspect, and beseech her to take off the spell she has put upon her innocent grandchild."

It seemed to me, indeed, that something like this was the best course we could pursue. But first it was necessary to ascertain more than what mere rumour or careless hearsay could tell. My thoughts turned to my uncle—he could advise me wisely—he ought to know all. I resolved to go to him without delay; but I did not choose to tell Mistress Clarke of all the visionary plans that flitted through my mind. I simply declared my intention of proceeding straight to London on Lucy's affairs. I bade her believe that my interest on the young lady's behalf was greater than ever, and that my whole time should be given up to her cause. I saw that Mistress Clarke distrusted me, because my mind was too full of thoughts for my words to flow freely. She sighed and shook her head, and said, "Well, it is all right!" in such a tone that it was an implied reproach. But I was firm and constant in my heart, and I took confidence from that.

I rode to London. I rode long days drawn out into the lovely summer nights: I could not rest. I reached London. I told my uncle all, though in the stir of the great city the horror had faded away, and I could hardly imagine that he would believe the account I gave him of the fearful double of Lucy which I had seen on the lonely moor-side. But my uncle had lived many years, and learnt many things; and, in the deep secrets of family history that had been confided to him, he had heard of cases of innocent people bewitched and taken possession of by evil spirits yet more fearful than Lucy's. For, as he said, to judge from all I told him, that resemblance had no power over her— she was too pure and good to be tainted by its evil, haunting presence. It had, in all probability, so my uncle conceived, tried to suggest wicked thoughts and to tempt to wicked actions but she, in her saintly maidenhood, had passed on undefiled by evil thought or deed. It could not touch her soul: but true, it set her apart from all sweet love or common human intercourse. My uncle threw himself with an energy more like six-and-twenty than sixty into the consideration of the whole case. He undertook the proving Lucy's descent, and volunteered to go and find out Mr. Gisborne, and obtain, firstly, the legal proofs of her descent from the Fitzgeralds of Kildoon, and, secondly, to try and hear all that he could respecting the working of the curse, and whether any and what means had been taken to exorcise that terrible appearance. For he told me of instances where, by prayers and long fasting, the evil possessor had been driven forth with howling and many cries from the body which it had come to inhabit; he spoke of those strange New England cases which had happened not so long before; of Mr. Defoe, who had written a book, wherein he had named many modes of subduing apparitions, and sending them back whence they came; and, lastly, he spoke low of dreadful ways of compelling witches to undo their witchcraft. But I could not endure to hear of those tortures and burnings. I said that Bridget was rather a wild and savage woman than a malignant witch; and, above all, that Lucy was of her kith and kin; and that, in putting her to the trial, by water or by fire, we should be torturing—it might be to the death—the ancestress of her we sought to redeem.

My uncle thought awhile, and then said, that in this last matter I was right—at any rate, it should not be tried, with his consent, till all other modes of remedy had failed; and he assented to my proposal that I should go myself and see Bridget, and tell her all.

In accordance with this, I went down once more to the wayside inn near Coldholme. It was late at night when I arrived there; and, while I supped, I inquired of the landlord more particulars as to Bridget's ways. Solitary and savage had been her life for many years. Wild and despotic were her words and manner to those few people who came across her path. The country-folk did her imperious bidding, because they feared to disobey. If they pleased her, they prospered; if, on the contrary, they neglected or traversed her behests, misfortune, small or great, fell on them and theirs. It was not detestation so much as an indefinable terror that she excited.

In the morning I went to see her. She was standing on the green outside her cottage, and received me with the sullen grandeur of a throneless queen. I read in her face that she recognized me, and that I was not unwelcome; but she stood silent till I had opened my errand.

"I have news of your daughter," said I, resolved to speak straight to all that I knew she felt of love, and not to spare her. "She is dead!"

The stern figure scarcely trembled, but her hand sought the support of the door-post.

"I knew that she was dead," said she, deep and low, and then was silent for an instant. "My tears that should have flowed for her were burnt up long years ago. Young man, tell me about her."

"Not yet," said I, having a strange power given me of confronting one, whom, nevertheless, in my secret soul I dreaded.

"You had once a little dog," I continued. The words called out in her more show of emotion than the intelligence of her daughter's death. She broke in upon my speech:-

"I had! It was hers—the last thing I had of hers—and it was shot for wantonness! It died in my arms. The man who killed that dog rues it to this day. For that dumb beast's blood, his best-beloved stands accursed."

Her eyes distended, as if she were in a trance and saw the working of her curse. Again I spoke:-

"O, woman!" I said, "that best-beloved, standing accursed before men, is your dead daughter's child."

The life, the energy, the passion, came back to the eyes with which she pierced through me, to see if I spoke truth; then, without another question or word, she threw herself on the ground with fearful vehemence, and clutched at the innocent daisies with convulsed hands.

"Bone of my bone! flesh of my flesh! have I cursed thee—and art thou accursed?"

So she moaned, as she lay prostrate in her great agony. I stood aghast at my own work. She did not hear my broken sentences; she asked no more, but the dumb confirmation which my sad looks had given that one fact, that her curse rested on her own daughter's child. The fear grew on me lest she should die in her strife of body and soul; and then might not Lucy remain under the spell as long as she lived?

Even at this moment, I saw Lucy coming through the woodland path that led to Bridget's cottage; Mistress Clarke was with her: I felt at my heart that it was she, by the balmy peace which the look of her sent over me, as she slowly advanced, a glad surprise shining out of her soft quiet eyes. That was as her gaze met mine. As her looks fell on the woman lying stiff, convulsed on the earth, they became full of tender pity; and she came forward to try and lift her up. Seating herself on the turf, she took Bridget's head into her lap; and, with gentle touches, she arranged the dishevelled gray hair streaming thick and wild from beneath her mutch.

"God help her!" murmured Lucy. "How she suffers!"

At her desire we sought for water; but when we returned, Bridget had recovered her wandering senses, and was kneeling with clasped hands before Lucy, gazing at that sweet sad face as though her troubled nature drank in health and peace from every moment's contemplation. A faint tinge on Lucy's pale cheeks showed me that she was aware of our return; otherwise it appeared as if she was conscious of her influence for good over the passionate and troubled woman kneeling before her, and would not willingly avert her grave and loving eyes from that wrinkled and careworn countenance.

Suddenly—in the twinkling of an eye—the creature appeared, there, behind Lucy; fearfully the same as to outward semblance, but kneeling exactly as Bridget knelt, and clasping her hands in jesting mimicry as Bridget clasped hers in her ecstasy that was deepening into a prayer. Mistress Clarke cried out—Bridget arose slowly, her gaze fixed on the creature beyond: drawing her breath with a hissing sound, never moving her terrible eyes, that were steady as stone, she made a dart at the phantom, and caught, as I had done, a mere handful of empty air. We saw no more of the creature—it vanished as suddenly as it came, but Bridget looked slowly on, as if watching some receding form. Lucy sat still, white, trembling, drooping—I think she would have swooned if I had not been there to uphold her. While I was attending to her, Bridget passed us, without a word to any one, and, entering her cottage, she barred herself in, and left us without.

All our endeavours were now directed to get Lucy back to the house where she had tarried the night before. Mistress Clarke told me that, not hearing from me (some letter must have miscarried), she had grown impatient and despairing, and had urged Lucy to the enterprise of coming to seek her grandmother; not telling her, indeed, of the dread reputation she possessed, or how we suspected her of having so fearfully blighted that innocent girl; but, at the same time, hoping much from the mysterious stirring of blood, which Mistress Clarke trusted in for the removal of the curse. They had come, by a different route from that which I had taken, to a village inn not far from Coldholme, only the night before. This was the first interview between ancestress and descendant.

All through the sultry noon I wandered along the tangled brush-wood of the old neglected forest, thinking where to turn for remedy in a matter so complicated and mysterious. Meeting a countryman, I asked my way to the nearest clergyman, and went, hoping to obtain some counsel from him. But he proved to be a coarse and common-minded man, giving no time or attention to the intricacies of a case, but dashing out a strong opinion involving immediate action. For instance, as soon as I named Bridget Fitzgerald, he exclaimed:-

"The Coldholme witch! the Irish papist! I'd have had her ducked long since but for that other papist, Sir Philip Tempest. He has had to threaten honest folk about here over and over again, or they'd have had her up before the justices for her black doings. And it's the law of the land that witches should be burnt! Ay, and of Scripture, too, sir! Yet you see a papist, if he's a rich squire, can overrule both law and Scripture. I'd carry a faggot myself to rid the country of her!"

Such a one could give me no help. I rather drew back what I had already said; and tried to make the parson forget it, by treating him to several pots of beer, in the village inn, to which we had adjourned for our conference at his suggestion. I left him as soon as I could, and returned to Coldholme, shaping my way past deserted Starkey Manor-house, and coming upon it by the back. At that side were the oblong remains of the old moat, the waters of which lay placid and motionless under the crimson rays of the setting

sun; with the forest-trees lying straight along each side, and their deep-green foliage mirrored to blackness in the burnished surface of the moat below—and the broken sun-dial at the end nearest the hall—and the heron, standing on one leg at the water's edge, lazily looking down for fish—the lonely and desolate house scarce needed the broken windows, the weeds on the door-sill, the broken shutter softly flapping to and fro in the twilight breeze, to fill up the picture of desertion and decay. I lingered about the place until the growing darkness warned me on. And then I passed along the path, cut by the orders of the last lady of Starkey Manor-House, that led me to Bridget's cottage. I resolved at once to see her; and, in spite of closed doors—it might be of resolved will—she should see me. So I knocked at her door, gently, loudly, fiercely. I shook it so vehemently that a length the old hinges gave way, and with a crash it fell inwards, leaving me suddenly face to face with Bridget—I, red, heated, agitated with my so long baffled efforts—she, stiff as any stone, standing right facing me, her eyes dilated with terror, her ashen lips trembling, but her body motionless. In her hands she held her crucifix, as if by that holy symbol she sought to oppose my entrance. At sight of me, her whole frame relaxed, and she sank back upon a chair. Some mighty tension had given way. Still her eyes looked fearfully into the gloom of the outer air, made more opaque by the glimmer of the lamp inside, which she had placed before the picture of the Virgin.
"Is she there?" asked Bridget, hoarsely.
"No! Who? I am alone. You remember me."
"Yes," replied she, still terror stricken. "But she—that creature— has been looking in upon me through that window all day long. I closed it up with my shawl; and then I saw her feet below the door, as long as it was light, and I knew she heard my very breathing—nay, worse, my very prayers; and I could not pray, for her listening choked the words ere they rose to my lips. Tell me, who is she?— what means that double girl I saw this morning? One had a look of my dead Mary; but the other curdled my blood, and yet it was the same!"
She had taken hold of my arm, as if to secure herself some human companionship. She shook all over with the slight, never-ceasing tremor of intense terror. I told her my tale as I have told it you, sparing none of the details.
How Mistress Clarke had informed me that the resemblance had driven Lucy forth from her father's house—how I had disbelieved, until, with mine own eyes, I had seen another Lucy standing behind my Lucy, the same in form and feature, but with the demon-soul looking out of the eyes. I told her all, I say, believing that she—whose curse was working so upon the life of her innocent grandchild—was the only person who could find the remedy and the redemption. When I had done, she sat silent for many minutes.

"You love Mary's child?" she asked.

"I do, in spite of the fearful working of the curse—I love her. Yet I shrink from her ever since that day on the moor-side. And men must shrink from one so accompanied; friends and lovers must stand afar off. Oh, Bridget Fitzgerald! loosen the curse! Set her free!"

"Where is she?"

I eagerly caught at the idea that her presence was needed, in order that, by some strange prayer or exorcism, the spell might be reversed.

"I will go and bring her to you," I exclaimed. Bridget tightened her hold upon my arm.

"Not so," said she, in a low, hoarse voice. "It would kill me to see her again as I saw her this morning. And I must live till I have worked my work. Leave me!" said she, suddenly, and again taking up the cross. "I defy the demon I have called up. Leave me to wrestle with it!"

She stood up, as if in an ecstasy of inspiration, from which all fear was banished. I lingered—why I can hardly tell—until once more she bade me begone. As I went along the forest way, I looked back, and saw her planting the cross in the empty threshold, where the door had been.

The next morning Lucy and I went to seek her, to bid her join her prayers with ours. The cottage stood open and wide to our gaze. No human being was there: the cross remained on the threshold, but Bridget was gone.

CHAPTER III.

What was to be done next? was the question that I asked myself. As for Lucy, she would fain have submitted to the doom that lay upon her. Her gentleness and piety, under the pressure of so horrible a life, seemed over-passive to me. She never complained. Mrs. Clarke complained more than ever. As for me, I was more in love with the real Lucy than ever; but I shrunk from the false similitude with an intensity proportioned to my love. I found out by instinct that Mrs. Clarke had occasional temptations to leave Lucy. The good lady's nerves were shaken, and, from what she said, I could almost have concluded that the object of the Double was to drive away from Lucy this last, and almost earliest friend. At times, I could scarcely bear to own it, but I myself felt inclined to turn recreant; and I would accuse Lucy of being too patient—too resigned. One after another, she won the little children of Coldholme. (Mrs. Clarke and she had resolved to stay there, for was it not as good a place as any other, to such as they? and did not all our faint hopes rest on Bridget—never seen or heard of now, but still we trusted to come back, or give some token?) So, as I say, one after another, the little children came about my Lucy, won by her soft tones, and her gentle smiles, and kind actions. Alas! one after another they fell away, and shrunk from her path with blanching terror; and we too surely guessed the reason why. It was the last drop. I could bear it no longer. I resolved no more to linger around the spot, but to go back to my uncle, and among the learned divines of the city of London, seek for some power whereby to annul the curse.

My uncle, meanwhile, had obtained all the requisite testimonials relating to Lucy's descent and birth, from the Irish lawyers, and from Mr. Gisborne. The latter gentleman had written from abroad (he was again serving in the Austrian army), a letter alternately passionately self-reproachful and stoically repellant. It was evident that when he thought of Mary—her short life— how he had wronged her, and of her violent death, he could hardly find words severe enough for his own conduct; and from this point of view, the curse that Bridget had laid upon him and his, was regarded by him as a prophetic doom, to the utterance of which she was moved by a Higher Power, working for the fulfilment of a deeper vengeance than for the death of the poor dog. But then, again, when he came to speak of his daughter, the repugnance which the conduct of the demoniac creature had produced in his mind, was but ill-disguised under a show of profound indifference as to Lucy's fate. One almost felt as if he would have been as content to put her out of existence, as he would have been to destroy some disgusting reptile that had invaded his chamber or his couch.

The great Fitzgerald property was Lucy's; and that was all—was nothing.

My uncle and I sat in the gloom of a London November evening, in our house in Ormond Street. I was out of health, and felt as if I were in an inextricable coil of misery. Lucy and I wrote to each other, but that was little; and we dared not see each other for dread of the fearful Third, who had more than once taken her place at our meetings. My uncle had, on the day I speak of, bidden prayers to be put up on the ensuing Sabbath in many a church and meeting-house in London, for one grievously tormented by an evil spirit. He had faith in prayers—I had none; I was fast losing faith in all things. So we sat, he trying to interest me in the old talk of other days, I oppressed by one thought—when our old servant, Anthony, opened the door, and, without speaking, showed in a very gentlemanly and prepossessing man, who had something remarkable about his dress, betraying his profession to be that of the Roman Catholic priesthood. He glanced at my uncle first, then at me. It was to me he bowed.

"I did not give my name," said he, "because you would hardly have recognised it; unless, sir, when, in the north, you heard of Father Bernard, the chaplain at Stoney Hurst?"

I remembered afterwards that I had heard of him, but at the time I had utterly forgotten it; so I professed myself a complete stranger to him; while my ever-hospitable uncle, although hating a papist as much as it was in his nature to hate anything, placed a chair for the visitor, and bade Anthony bring glasses, and a fresh jug of claret.

Father Bernard received this courtesy with the graceful ease and pleasant acknowledgement which belongs to a man of the world. Then he turned to scan me with his keen glance. After some alight conversation, entered into on his part, I am certain, with an intention of discovering on what terms of confidence I stood with my uncle, he paused, and said gravely -

"I am sent here with a message to you, sir, from a woman to whom you have shown kindness, and who is one of my penitents, in Antwerp—one Bridget Fitzgerald."

"Bridget Fitzgerald!" exclaimed I. "In Antwerp? Tell me, sir, all that you can about her."

"There is much to be said," he replied. "But may I inquire if this gentleman—if your uncle is acquainted with the particulars of which you and I stand informed?"

"All that I know, he knows," said I, eagerly laying my hand on my uncle's arm, as he made a motion as if to quit the room.

"Then I have to speak before two gentlemen who, however they may differ from me in faith, are yet fully impressed with the fact that there are evil powers going about continually to take cognizance of our evil thoughts: and, if their Master gives them power, to bring them into overt action. Such is my theory of the nature of that sin, which I dare not disbelieve—as some sceptics would have us do—the sin of witchcraft. Of this deadly sin, you and I are aware, Bridget Fitzgerald has been guilty. Since you saw her last, many prayers have been offered in our churches, many masses sung, many penances undergone, in order that, if God and the holy saints so willed it, her sin might be blotted out. But it has not been so willed."

"Explain to me," said I, "who you are, and how you come connected with Bridget. Why is she at Antwerp? I pray you, sir, tell me more. If I am impatient, excuse me; I am ill and feverish, and in consequence bewildered."

There was something to me inexpressibly soothing in the tone of voice with which he began to narrate, as it were from the beginning, his acquaintance with Bridget.

"I had known Mr. and Mrs. Starkey during their residence abroad, and so it fell out naturally that, when I came as chaplain to the Sherburnes at Stoney Hurst, our acquaintance was renewed; and thus I became the confessor of the whole family, isolated as they were from the offices of the Church, Sherburne being their nearest neighbour who professed the true faith. Of course, you are aware that facts revealed in confession are sealed as in the grave; but I learnt enough of Bridget's character to be convinced that I had to do with no common woman; one powerful for good as for evil. I believe that I was able to give her spiritual assistance from time to time, and that she looked upon me as a servant of that Holy Church, which has such wonderful power of moving men's hearts, and relieving them of the burden of their sins. I have known her cross the moors on the wildest nights of storm, to confess and be absolved; and then she would return, calmed and subdued, to her daily work about her mistress, no one witting where she had been during the hours that most passed in sleep upon their beds. After her daughter's departure—after Mary's mysterious disappearance—I had to impose many a long penance, in order to wash away the sin of impatient repining that was fast leading her into the deeper guilt of blasphemy. She set out on that long journey of which you have possibly heard—that fruitless journey in search of Mary—and during her absence, my superiors ordered my return to my former duties at Antwerp, and for many years I heard no more of Bridget.

"Not many months ago, as I was passing homewards in the evening, along one of the streets near St. Jacques, leading into the Meer Straet, I saw a woman sitting crouched up under the shrine of the Holy Mother of Sorrows. Her hood was drawn over her head, so that the shadow caused by the light of the lamp above fell deep over her face; her hands were clasped round her knees. It was evident that she was some one in hopeless trouble, and as such it was my duty to stop and speak. I naturally addressed her first in Flemish, believing her to be one of the lower class of inhabitants. She shook her head, but did not look up. Then I tried French, and she replied in that language, but speaking it so indifferently, that I was sure she was either English or Irish, and consequently spoke to her in my own native tongue. She recognized my voice; and, starting up, caught at my robes, dragging me before the blessed shrine, and throwing herself down, and forcing me, as much by her evident desire as by her action, to kneel beside her, she exclaimed:

"'O Holy Virgin! you will never hearken to me again, but hear him; for you know him of old, that he does your bidding, and strives to heal broken hearts. Hear him!'

"She turned to me.

"'She will hear you, if you will only pray. She never hears ME: she and all the saints in heaven cannot hear my prayers, for the Evil One carries them off, as he carried that first away. O, Father Bernard, pray for me!'

"I prayed for one in sore distress, of what nature I could not say; but the Holy Virgin would know. Bridget held me fast, gasping with eagerness at the sound of my words. When I had ended, I rose, and, making the sign of the Cross over her, I was going to bless her in the name of the Holy Church, when she shrank away like some terrified creature, and said -

"'I am guilty of deadly sin, and am not shriven.'

"'Arise, my daughter,' said I, 'and come with me.' And I led the way into one of the confessionals of St. Jaques.

"She knelt; I listened. No words came. The evil powers had stricken her dumb, as I heard afterwards they had many a time before, when she approached confession.

"She was too poor to pay for the necessary forms of exorcism; and hitherto those priests to whom she had addressed herself were either so ignorant of the meaning of her broken French, or her Irish- English, or else esteemed her to be one crazed—as, indeed, her wild and excited manner might easily have led any one to think—that they had neglected the sole means of loosening her tongue, so that she might confess her deadly sin, and, after due penance, obtain absolution. But I knew Bridget of old, and felt that she was a penitent sent to me. I went through those holy offices appointed by our Church for the relief of such a case. I was the more bound to do this, as I found that she had come to Antwerp for the sole purpose of discovering me, and making confession to me. Of the nature of that fearful confession I am forbidden to speak. Much of it you know; possibly all.

"It now remains for her to free herself from mortal guilt, and to set others free from the consequences thereof. No prayers, no masses, will ever do it, although they may strengthen her with that strength by which alone acts of deepest love and purest self-devotion may be performed. Her words of passion, and cries for revenge—her unholy prayers could never reach the ears of the holy saints! Other powers intercepted them, and wrought so that the curses thrown up to heaven have fallen on her own flesh and blood; and so, through her very strength of love, have bruised and crushed her heart. Henceforward her former self must be buried,—yea, buried quick, if need be,—but never more to make sign, or utter cry on earth! She has become a Poor Clare, in order that, by perpetual penance and constant service of others, she may at length so act as to obtain final absolution and rest for her soul. Until then, the innocent must suffer. It is to plead for the innocent that I come to you; not in the name of the witch, Bridget Fitzgerald, but of the penitent and servant of all men, the Poor Clare, Sister Magdalen."

"Sir," said I, "I listen to your request with respect; only I may tell you it is not needed to urge me to do all that I can on behalf of one, love for whom is part of my very life. If for a time I have absented myself from her, it is to think and work for her redemption. I, a member of the English Church—my uncle, a Puritan—pray morning and night for her by name: the congregations of London, on the next Sabbath, will pray for one unknown, that she may be set free from the Powers of Darkness. Moreover, I must tell you, sir, that those evil ones touch not the great calm of her soul. She lives her own pure and loving life, unharmed and untainted, though all men fall off from her. I would I could have her faith!"

My uncle now spoke.

"Nephew," said he, "it seems to me that this gentleman, although professing what I consider an erroneous creed, has touched upon the right point in exhorting Bridget to acts of love and mercy, whereby to wipe out her sin of hate and vengeance. Let us strive after our fashion, by almsgiving and visiting of the needy and fatherless, to make our prayers acceptable. Meanwhile, I myself will go down into the north, and take charge of the maiden. I am too old to be daunted by man or demon. I will bring her to this house as to a home; and let the Double come if it will! A company of godly divines shall give it the meeting, and we will try issue."

The kindly, brave old man! But Father Bernard sat on musing.

"All hate," said he, "cannot be quenched in her heart; all Christian forgiveness cannot have entered into her soul, or the demon would have lost its power. You said, I think, that her grandchild was still tormented?"

"Still tormented!" I replied, sadly, thinking of Mistress Clarke's last letter—

He rose to go. We afterwards heard that the occasion of his coming to London was a secret political mission on behalf of the Jacobites. Nevertheless, he was a good and a wise man.

Months and months passed away without any change. Lucy entreated my uncle to leave her where she was,—dreading, as I learnt, lest if she came, with her fearful companion, to dwell in the same house with me, that my love could not stand the repeated shocks to which I should be doomed. And this she thought from no distrust of the strength of my affection, but from a kind of pitying sympathy for the terror to the nerves which she clearly observed that the demoniac visitation caused in all.

I was restless and miserable. I devoted myself to good works; but I performed them from no spirit of love, but solely from the hope of reward and payment, and so the reward was never granted. At length, I asked my uncle's leave to travel; and I went forth, a wanderer, with no distincter end than that of many another wanderer—to get away from myself. A strange impulse led me to Antwerp, in spite of the wars and commotions then raging in the Low Countries—or rather, perhaps, the very craving to become interested in something external, led me into the thick of the struggle then going on with the Austrians. The cities of Flanders were all full at that time of civil disturbances and rebellions, only kept down by force, and the presence of an Austrian garrison in every place.

I arrived in Antwerp, and made inquiry for Father Bernard. He was away in the country for a day or two. Then I asked my way to the Convent of Poor Clares; but, being healthy and prosperous, I could only see the dim, pent-up, gray walls, shut closely in by narrow streets, in the lowest part of the town. My landlord told me, that had I been stricken by some loathsome disease, or in desperate case of any kind, the Poor Clares would have taken me, and tended me. He spoke of them as an order of mercy of the strictest kind, dressing scantily in the coarsest materials, going barefoot, living on what the inhabitants of Antwerp chose to bestow, and sharing even those fragments and crumbs with the poor and helpless that swarmed all around; receiving no letters or communication with the outer world; utterly dead to everything but the alleviation of suffering. He smiled at my inquiring whether I could get speech of one of them; and told me that they were even forbidden to speak for the purposes of begging their daily food; while yet they lived, and fed others upon what was given in charity.

"But," exclaimed I, "supposing all men forgot them! Would they quietly lie down and die, without making sign of their extremity?"

"If such were the rule the Poor Clares would willingly do it; but their founder appointed a remedy for such extreme cases as you suggest. They have a bell—'tis but a small one, as I have heard, and has yet never been rung in the memory man: when the Poor Clares have been without food for twenty-four hours, they may ring this bell, and then trust to our good people of Antwerp for rushing to the rescue of the Poor Clares, who have taken such blessed care of us in all our straits."

It seemed to me that such rescue would be late in the day; but I did not say what I thought. I rather turned the conversation, by asking my landlord if he knew, or had ever heard, anything of a certain Sister Magdalen.

"Yes," said he, rather under his breath, "news will creep out, even from a convent of Poor Clares. Sister Magdalen is either a great sinner or a great saint. She does more, as I have heard, than all the other nuns put together; yet, when last month they would fain have made her mother-superior, she begged rather that they would place her below all the rest, and make her the meanest servant of all."

"You never saw her?" asked I.

"Never," he replied.

I was weary of waiting for Father Bernard, and yet I lingered in Antwerp. The political state of things became worse than ever, increased to its height by the scarcity of food consequent on many deficient harvests. I saw groups of fierce, squalid men, at every corner of the street, glaring out with wolfish eyes at my sleek skin and handsome clothes.

At last Father Bernard returned. We had a long conversation, in which he told me that, curiously enough, Mr. Gisborne, Lucy's father, was serving in one of the Austrian regiments, then in garrison at Antwerp. I asked Father Bernard if he would make us acquainted; which he consented to do. But, a day or two afterwards, he told me that, on hearing my name, Mr. Gisborne had declined responding to any advances on my part, saying he had adjured his country, and hated his countrymen.

Probably he recollected my name in connection with that of his daughter Lucy. Anyhow, it was clear enough that I had no chance of making his acquaintance. Father Bernard confirmed me in my suspicions of the hidden fermentation, for some coming evil, working among the "blouses" of Antwerp, and he would fain have had me depart from out the city; but I rather craved the excitement of danger, and stubbornly refused to leave.

One day, when I was walking with him in the Place Verte, he bowed to an

Austrian officer, who was crossing towards the cathedral.

"That is Mr. Gisborne," said he, as soon as the gentleman was past.

I turned to look at the tall, slight figure of the officer. He carried himself in a stately manner, although he was past middle age, and from his years might have had some excuse for a slight stoop. As I looked at the man, he turned round, his eyes met mine, and I saw his face. Deeply lined, sallow, and scathed was that countenance; scarred by passion as well as by the fortunes of war. 'Twas but a moment our eyes met. We each turned round, and went on our separate way.

But his whole appearance was not one to be easily forgotten; the thorough appointment of the dress, and evident thought bestowed on it, made but an incongruous whole with the dark, gloomy expression of his countenance. Because he was Lucy's father, I sought instinctively to meet him everywhere. At last he must have become aware of my pertinacity, for he gave me a haughty scowl whenever I passed him. In one of these encounters, however, I chanced to be of some service to him. He was turning the corner of a street, and came suddenly on one of the groups of discontented Flemings of whom I have spoken. Some words were exchanged, when my gentleman out with his sword, and with a slight but skilful cut drew blood from one of those who had insulted him, as he fancied, though I was too far off to hear the words. They would all have fallen upon him had I not rushed forwards and raised the cry, then well known in Antwerp, of rally, to the Austrian soldiers who were perpetually patrolling the streets, and who came in numbers to the rescue. I think that neither Mr. Gisborne nor the mutinous group of plebeians owed me much gratitude for my interference. He had planted himself against a wall, in a skilful attitude of fence, ready with his bright glancing rapier to do battle with all the heavy, fierce, unarmed men, some six or seven in number. But when his own soldiers came up, he sheathed his sword; and, giving some careless word of command, sent them away again, and continued his saunter all alone down the street, the workmen snarling in his rear, and more than half-inclined to fall on me for my cry for rescue. I cared not if they did, my life seemed so dreary a burden just then; and, perhaps, it was this daring loitering among them that prevented their attacking me. Instead, they suffered me to fall into conversation with them; and I heard some of their grievances. Sore and heavy to be borne were they, and no wonder the sufferers were savage and desperate.

The man whom Gisborne had wounded across his face would fain have got out of me the name of his aggressor, but I refused to tell it. Another of the group heard his inquiry, and made answer—"I know the man. He is one Gisborne, aide-de-camp to the General-Commandant. I know him well."

He began to tell some story in connection with Gisborne in a low and muttering voice; and while he was relating a tale, which I saw excited their evil blood, and which they evidently wished me not to hear, I sauntered away and back to my lodgings.

That night Antwerp was in open revolt. The inhabitants rose in rebellion against their Austrian masters. The Austrians, holding the gates of the city, remained at first pretty quiet in the citadel; only, from time to time, the boom of the great cannon swept sullenly over the town. But if they expected the disturbance to die away, and spend itself in a few hours' fury, they were mistaken. In a day or two, the rioters held possession of the principal municipal buildings. Then the Austrians poured forth in bright flaming array, calm and smiling, as they marched to the posts assigned, as if the fierce mob were no more to them then the swarms of buzzing summer flies. Their practised manoeuvres, their well-aimed shot, told with terrible effect; but in the place of one slain rioter, three sprang up of his blood to avenge his loss. But a deadly foe, a ghastly ally of the Austrians, was at work. Food, scarce and dear for months, was now hardly to be obtained at any price. Desperate efforts were being made to bring provisions into the city, for the rioters had friends without. Close to the city port, nearest to the Scheldt, a great struggle took place. I was there, helping the rioters, whose cause I had adopted. We had a savage encounter with the Austrians. Numbers fell on both sides: I saw them lie bleeding for a moment: then a volley of smoke obscured them; and when it cleared away, they were dead—trampled upon or smothered, pressed down and hidden by the freshly-wounded whom those last guns had brought low. And then a gray-robed and grey-veiled figure came right across the flashing guns and stooped over some one, whose life-blood was ebbing away; sometimes it was to give him drink from cans which they carried slung at their sides; sometimes I saw the cross held above a dying man, and rapid prayers were being uttered, unheard by men in that hellish din and clangour, but listened to by One above. I saw all this as in a dream: the reality of that stern time was battle and carnage. But I knew that these gray figures, their bare feet all wet with blood, and their faces hidden by their veils, were the Poor Clares—sent forth now because dire agony was abroad and imminent danger at hand. Therefore, they left their cloistered shelter, and came into that thick and evil melee.

Close to me—driven past me by the struggle of many fighters—came the Antwerp burgess with the scarce-healed scar upon his face; and in an instant more, he was thrown by the press upon the Austrian officer Gisborne, and ere either had recovered the shock, the burgess had recognized his opponent.

"Ha! the Englishman Gisborne!" he cried, and threw himself upon him with redoubled fury. He had struck him hard—the Englishman was down; when out of the smoke came a dark-gray figure, and threw herself right under the uplifted flashing sword. The burgess's arm stood arrested. Neither

Austrians nor Anversois willingly harmed the Poor Clares.

"Leave him to me!" said a low stern voice. "He is mine enemy—mine for many years."

Those words were the last I heard. I myself was struck down by a bullet. I remember nothing more for days. When I came to myself, I was at the extremity of weakness, and was craving for food to recruit my strength. My landlord sat watching me. He, too, looked pinched and shrunken; he had heard of my wounded state, and sought me out. Yes! the struggle still continued, but the famine was sore: and some, he had heard, had died for lack of food. The tears stood in his eyes as he spoke. But soon he shook off his weakness, and his natural cheerfulness returned. Father Bernard had been to see me—no one else. (Who should, indeed?) Father Bernard would come back that afternoon—he had promised. But Father Bernard never came, although I was up and dressed, and looking eagerly for him.

My landlord brought me a meal which he had cooked himself: of what it was composed he would not say, but it was most excellent, and with every mouthful I seemed to gain strength. The good man sat looking at my evident enjoyment with a happy smile of sympathy; but, as my appetite became satisfied, I began to detect a certain wistfulness in his eyes, as if craving for the food I had so nearly devoured—for, indeed, at that time I was hardly aware of the extent of the famine. Suddenly, there was a sound of many rushing feet past our window. My landlord opened one of the sides of it, the better to learn what was going on. Then we heard a faint, cracked, tinkling bell, coming shrill upon the air, clear and distinct from all other sounds. "Holy Mother!" exclaimed my landlord, "the Poor Clares!"

He snatched up the fragments of my meal, and crammed them into my hands, bidding me follow. Down stairs he ran, clutching at more food, as the women of his house eagerly held it out to him; and in a moment we were in the street, moving along with the great current, all tending towards the Convent of the Poor Clares. And still, as if piercing our ears with its inarticulate cry, came the shrill tinkle of the bell. In that strange crowd were old men trembling and sobbing, as they carried their little pittance of food; women with tears running down their cheeks, who had snatched up what provisions they had in the vessels in which they stood, so that the burden of these was in many cases much greater than that which they contained; children, with flushed faces, grasping tight the morsel of bitten cake or bread, in their eagerness to carry it safe to the help of the Poor Clares; strong men—yea, both Anversois and Austrians—pressing onward with set teeth, and no word spoken; and over all, and through all, came that sharp tinkle—that cry for help in extremity.

We met the first torrent of people returning with blanched and piteous faces: they were issuing out of the convent to make way for the offerings of others. "Haste, haste!" said they. "A Poor Clare is dying! A Poor Clare is

dead for hunger! God forgive us and our city!"
We pressed on. The stream bore us along where it would. We were carried through refectories, bare and crumbless; into cells over whose doors the conventual name of the occupant was written. Thus it was that I, with others, was forced into Sister Magdalen's cell. On her couch lay Gisborne, pale unto death, but not dead. By his side was a cup of water, and a small morsel of mouldy bread, which he had pushed out of his reach, and could not move to obtain. Over against his bed were these words, copied in the English version "Therefore, if thine enemy hunger, feed him; if he thirst, give him drink."
Some of us gave him of our food, and left him eating greedily, like some famished wild animal. For now it was no longer the sharp tinkle, but that one solemn toll, which in all Christian countries tells of the passing of the spirit out of earthly life into eternity; and again a murmur gathered and grew, as of many people speaking with awed breath, "A Poor Clare is dying! a Poor Clare is dead!"
Borne along once more by the motion of the crowd, we were carried into the chapel belonging to the Poor Clares. On a bier before the high altar, lay a woman—lay Sister Magdalen—lay Bridget Fitzgerald. By her side stood Father Bernard, in his robes of office, and holding the crucifix on high while he pronounced the solemn absolution of the Church, as to one who had newly confessed herself of deadly sin. I pushed on with passionate force, till I stood close to the dying woman, as she received extreme unction amid the breathless and awed hush of the multitude around. Her eyes were glazing, her limbs were stiffening; but when the rite was over and finished, she raised her gaunt figure slowly up, and her eyes brightened to a strange intensity of joy, as, with the gesture of her finger and the trance-like gleam of her eye, she seemed like one who watched the disappearance of some loathed and fearful creature.
"She is freed from the curse!" said she, as she fell back dead.

THE POOR CLARE

Printed in Great Britain
by Amazon